ISBN 978-1-60091-821-6

Book design by: YJ Studios

Audiobook produced by: HillelKAPS Productions (www.HillelKaps.com)
Audiobook recorded @ Uptop Studios (Monsey, NY)
Engineered and Narrated by: Hillel Kapnick

Additional Voices:
Chaim Levi
Shmuel Solomon
Yehuda Kapnick
Ahuva Shira Kapnick
Gila Kapnick

Distributed by:
Israel Bookshop Publications
501 Prospect Street
Lakewood, NJ 08701

Tel: (732) 901-3009
Fax: (732) 901-4012
www.israelbookshoppublications.com
info@israelbookshoppublications.com

Printed in Bulgaria

Distributed in Israel by:
Tfutza Publications
P.O.B. 50036
Beitar Illit 90500
972-2-650-9400

Distributed in Europe by:
Lehmanns
Unit E Viking Industrial Park
Rolling Mill Road,
Jarrow, Tyne & Wear NE32 3DP
44-191-430-0333

Distributed in Australia by:
Gold's Book and Gift Company
3-13 William Street
Balaclava 3183
613-9527-8775

Distributed in South Africa by:
Kollel Bookshop
Northfield Centre
17 Northfield Avenue
Glenhazel 2192
27-11-440-6679

MIDDOSMAN
PERFECTING MY PATIENCE

By Esther Ornstein

Illustrations by Yoel Judowitz and the YJ Studios Team

Audio book by Hillel Kapnick

Mr. Yetzer Horah hopped in the elevator with his pogo stick. He heard there was a birthday party on the roof today. Just the perfect place to make some trouble.

3

As Mr. Yetzer Horah got out of the elevator, he left his pogo stick in the middle of the open door. Now the elevator could not close and go back down.

This party looked exciting. He stayed behind the plants and watched carefully. Mr. Yetzer Horah was waiting for the right moment.

Shimon was turning three today, and he was having an *upsherin*. Mr. Yetzer Horah noticed that Shimon's older brother, Yehuda, was having a lot of fun. He and his friend Bentzy were jumping in the bouncy house together.

After a few minutes, Bentzy and Yehuda got thirsty. They went over to the table with all the drinks and tried to get the cups. But the cups were all the way in the middle of the table, and they couldn't reach them.

Yehuda said, "Hey, Bentzy, let's go find my mommy. She'll give us a drink."

Yehuda looked all over for his mommy. When he finally found her, he asked, "Mommy? Can you please give me and Bentzy a drink? We are so, so-o-o thirsty!"

"Sure, boys! I'd love to get you a drink. Just give me a few minutes, and I'll come to the drinks table to help you," Mommy replied.

Mr. Yetzer Horah came out from behind the plants and snuck up next to Yehuda. This was the perfect moment!

"Yehuda, you're so thirsty, you can't wait even one minute!" whispered Mr. Yetzer Horah. "No way! Tell Mommy you need a drink *right now*!"

Yehuda looked at Mr. Yetzer Horah. Yehuda looked at Mommy. Without even thinking, he walked closer to Mommy and started whining.

"Mommy, I am so, so, so, so thirsty! I can't wait. I just can't. I need a drink right now!"

Mr. Yetzer Horah did a happy little dance. He was helping Yehuda not have any patience! Yippee!

9

MiddosMan was driving in his MiddosCar. He was just coming back from a call. As he was pulling into the garage at Middos Headquarters, his radio started beeping. Oh, no! What did Mr. Yetzer Horah do this time?

"MiddosMan Headquarters here," he heard someone calling on his radio. "MiddosMan? We have a patience emergency at the top of an apartment building about five blocks away. Can you make it?"

MiddosMan responded, "MiddosMan ready for action! Please send me the address, and I'm on my way!"

MiddosMan flipped on his sirens and drove off.

MiddosMan parked right in front of the building and ran inside. He pushed the elevator button and waited. A bubby passed by. "Oh, hello, MiddosMan," the bubby said. "You know, it seems like the elevator is broken. Someone is coming to fix it in about half an hour."

MiddosMan thought. If he stayed there until the elevator was fixed, then Mr. Yetzer Horah would have thirty extra minutes to make more trouble. If Middosman ran up to the roof using the steps, that would also leave Mr. Yetzer Horah with too much time! What would be the quickest way for him to reach the rooftop?

Good thing Middosman was wearing his fly shoes today! He reached toward his shoes and pulled the string. Air blasted out and pushed Middosman up toward the roof.

Whoo-hoo! Up, up, up went MiddosMan!
As he flew up, he sang this song:
I fly, I fly, as fast as I can,
I fly to help, 'cause I'm MiddosMan!

MiddosMan went all the way to the rooftop. He landed right near the plants. And who do you think was standing right there?

Mr. Yetzer Horah looked up, and his mouth dropped open. How had MiddosMan gotten there so quickly? Mr. Yetzer Horah scooted off to the side to see what would happen next.

MiddosMan got to Yehuda just in time. He was about to start whining again.

MiddosMan spoke softly. "Yehuda, this looks like a really fun *upsherin* party! What is your favorite part of it?"

"Middosman, it is a really exciting party, and I had so much fun jumping in the bouncy house with my friend Bentzy. But I got so, so thirsty from all that bouncing, and now I can't even wait a minute for my mother to help me get a drink!"

"I see," said Middosman. "It's hard to be patient. But it looks like your mother is wiping your baby sister's sticky hands right now."

Yehuda looked at his mother. His baby sister's hands were really sticky.

So that's why Mommy can't get me a drink right this second, he realized. She's busy with my little sister. But still... I really need a drink badly!

Hmm. Yehuda continued thinking. Maybe he could wait just a little bit longer to get his drink. He turned to look at Mommy again, but she wasn't standing in that spot anymore.

"Yehuda, Bentzy, here are your drinks!" Mommy called. She had come to the drinks table already!

"Thank you!" the boys called out to Yehuda's mother.
Both boys made a beautiful *brachah* together.

After Yehuda took a drink, Middosman said, "Yehuda, there are many times when we have to be patient and wait a while for something. It's never easy. Can you think of another time when you had to be patient?"

Yehuda nodded. "Last week, when I was doing my homework, I needed some help, but my mother was busy making supper. I waited until she finished cooking the noodles. Then she helped me."

Bentzy added in, "Last Friday, our *rebbi* gave out my favorite Shabbos party treat: chocolate cream cookies! I really wanted to be first to get, but I had to wait a little while, because my seat is close to the back. I waited patiently, but it wasn't so easy."

Yehuda said, "When Bentzy got a new football, I was excited to use it. Then, when I came over, the neighbors were in middle of using it. So I waited a few minutes until it was my turn!"

MiddosMan smiled. "Those are all great examples of having patience, boys!"

Bentzy added, "Yehuda's mommy really only needed a little time. The baby was a mess."

"Right, my sister was just so sticky from that ice pop!" Yehuda giggled.

MiddosMan agreed. "Sometimes people just need a little time to finish something before they can help us or give us their attention. Waiting patiently can really help everyone."

Yehuda looked up. "I feel bad that I whined and wasn't being patient before. I'm going to say sorry to Mommy."

Yehuda apologized to Mommy and gave her a big hug.

Mr. Yetzer Horah felt himself shrinking. As he became smaller
and smaller, he quickly left the party area.

MiddosMan said "mazel tov" to Shimon on turning three. Then he asked all the guests at the *upsherin*, "Who wants to hear a new song about patience?"

Everyone cheered!

MiddosMan went up to the stage where Yehuda's cousin, Zalmen, was playing on a keyboard. He asked Zalmen to play some music for his new song.

27

MiddosMan stood near the microphone and started singing.

Sometimes it's hard to wait,
But if you do, it'll feel great.
Patience is the name of the game!

Sometimes we want it now.
Still, we can wait somehow.
Patience is the name of the game!

If Daddy is busy, we can wait—yes, we could;
Patience is a middah that is really good.
When Mommy needs a minute, we can say, "Okay!"
We can have patience; we can have it today!

All the guests clapped.

Yehuda smiled at MiddosMan. He thought to himself, *I'm really going to work on having more patience. It's not always easy, but I'm going to try very hard. I will not listen to Mr. Yetzer Horah!*

Yehuda and Bentzy walked MiddosMan back to the elevator. It was working now.

"Goodbye, MiddosMan," called out Bentzy.

"Goodbye, MiddosMan," said Yehuda. "Thank you for coming and helping me!"